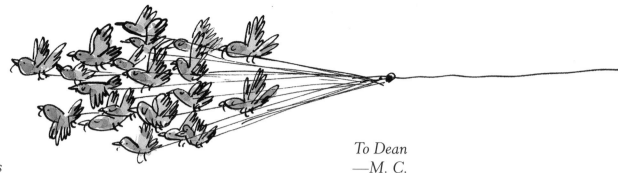

To Niki,
Mailer of Elephants
—P. S.

To Dean
—M. C.

Text copyright © 2015 Philip C. Stead
Illustration copyright © 2015 Matthew Cordell
A Neal Porter Book
Published by Roaring Brook Press
Roaring Brook Press is a division of Holtzbrinck Publishing Holdings Limited Partnership
175 Fifth Avenue, New York, New York 10010
The artwork for this book was created using pen and ink with watercolor.
mackids.com

Library of Congress Cataloging-in-Publication Data

Stead, Philip Christian.
  Special delivery / Philip C. Stead ; illustrated by Matthew Cordell.
    pages cm
  Summary: "A little girl goes on a long journey to delivery an elephant
to her great aunt"— Provided by publisher.
  ISBN 978-1-59643-931-3 (hardback)
  [1. Voyages and travels—Fiction. 2. Elephants—Fiction.] I. Cordell,
Matthew, 1975– illustrator. II. Title.
  PZ7.S808566Spe 2015
  [E]—dc23
                                                    2014009900

Roaring Brook Press books may be purchased for business or promotional use. For information
on bulk purchases please contact Macmillan Corporate and Premium Sales Department
at (800) 221-7945 x5442 or by email at specialmarkets@macmillan.com.

First edition 2015
Book design by Philip C. Stead and Matthew Cordell
Printed in China by
Toppan Leefung Printing Ltd.,
Dongguan City, Guangdong Province

1 3 5 7 9 10 8 6 4 2

Special Delivery

written by
Philip C. Stead

illustrated by
Matthew Cordell

A Neal Porter Book Roaring Brook Press New York

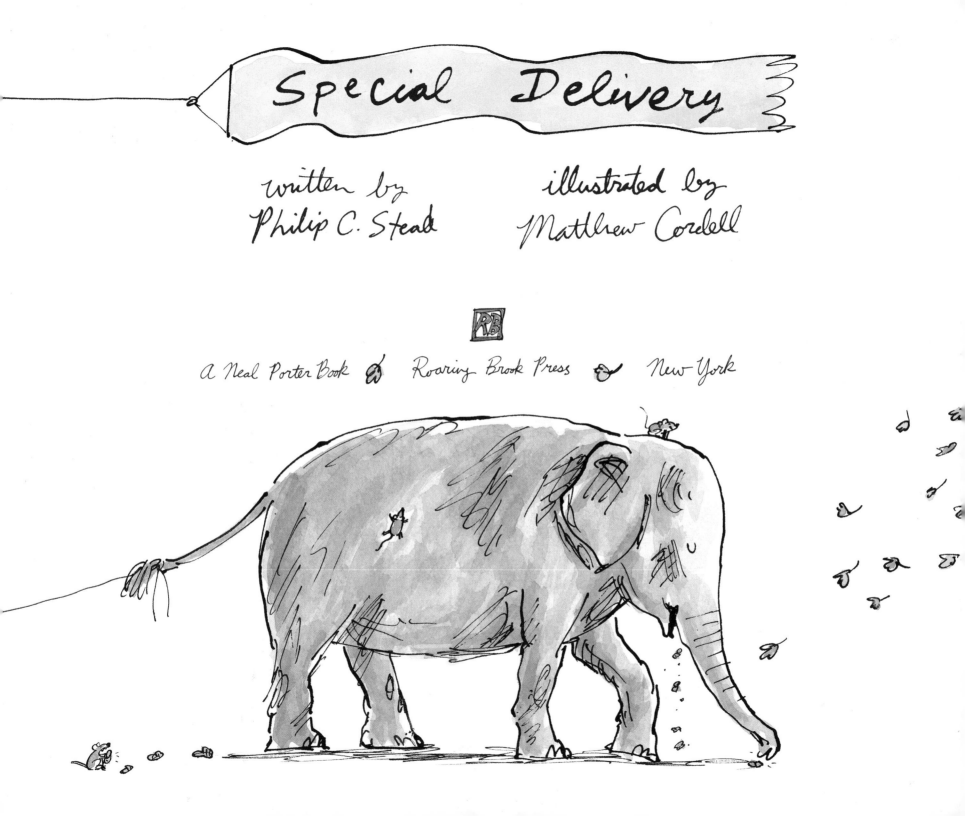

"Where are you going?"

"Where do you think? You don't just drop an elephant in the mailbox. You've got to go to the . . .

"Hey, Sadie."

"Hey, Jim. I'd like to mail this elephant, please, to my Great-Aunt Josephine—
who lives almost completely alone and could really use the company."

"Please be gentle with him. Do not bend him, or drop him, or
shake him much at all. He is fragile and very easily might break."

"You'll need a lot of stamps, Sadie."

"How many?"

"This many."

"You may have to find another way!"

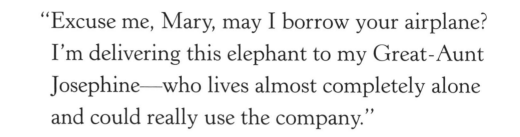

"Excuse me, Mary, may I borrow your airplane? I'm delivering this elephant to my Great-Aunt Josephine—who lives almost completely alone and could really use the company."

"Of course, Sadie. But elephants are heavy.
You'll need lots of fuel before you . . .

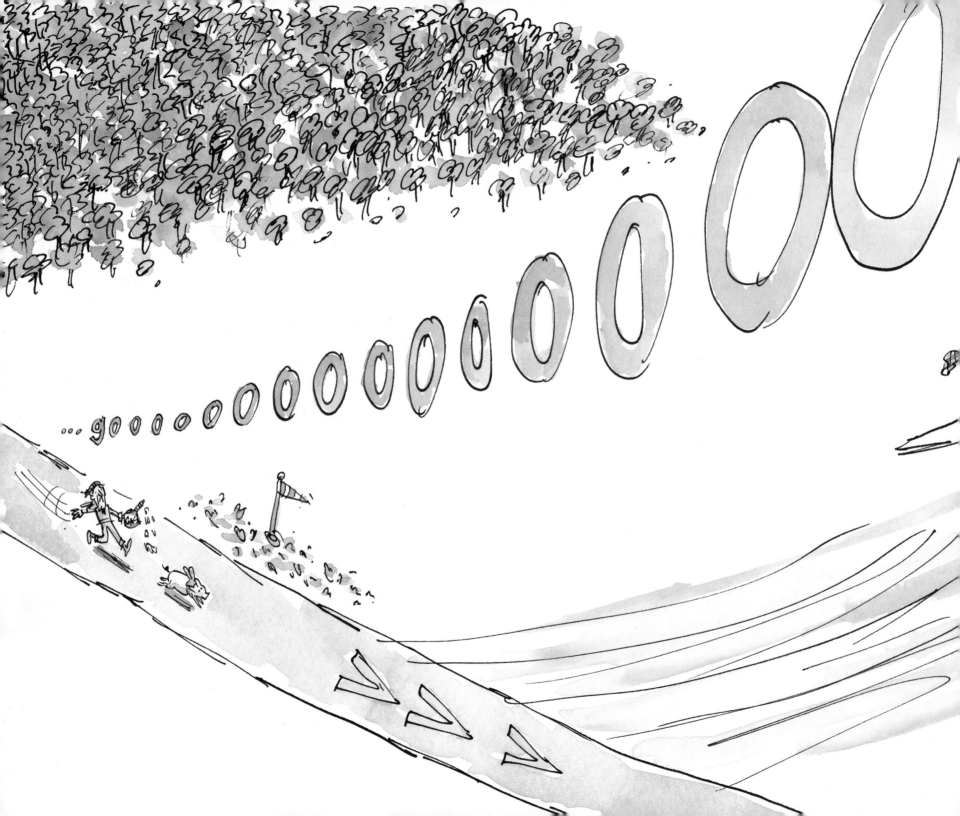

"Oh, hello, Alligator. Will you guide me down the river, please?
I'm delivering this elephant to my Great-Aunt Josephine—
who lives almost completely alone and could really use the company."

"Goodbye, Alligator, and thank you. Someday I'll mail you a real letter and inside will be a giant stick of bubble gum."

"A train will get us there quickly, and anyway it's nice to see new things."

"And even if we're robbed by bandits it's okay because . . .

we'll join the bandits . . .

and have a great time . . .

till one of us says . . .

'Thank you, Bandits, but I prefer ice cream now.'"

"Ice cream sandwiches for everyone, please.
And also will you deliver us to my Great-Aunt Josephine—

dee doo dee doo dee doo dee doo de

who lives almost completely alone and as you can see . . .

dee
doo dee
doo dee
doo dee
doo dee
doo dee

. . . could really use the company."

to: AUNT J.

from: SADIE
to: AUNT J.

"Would you like hot chocolate, Sadie?"
"Yes, Aunt J., thank you. But not until I mail this letter."

Chugga Chugga Chugga BEANS BEANS BEANS